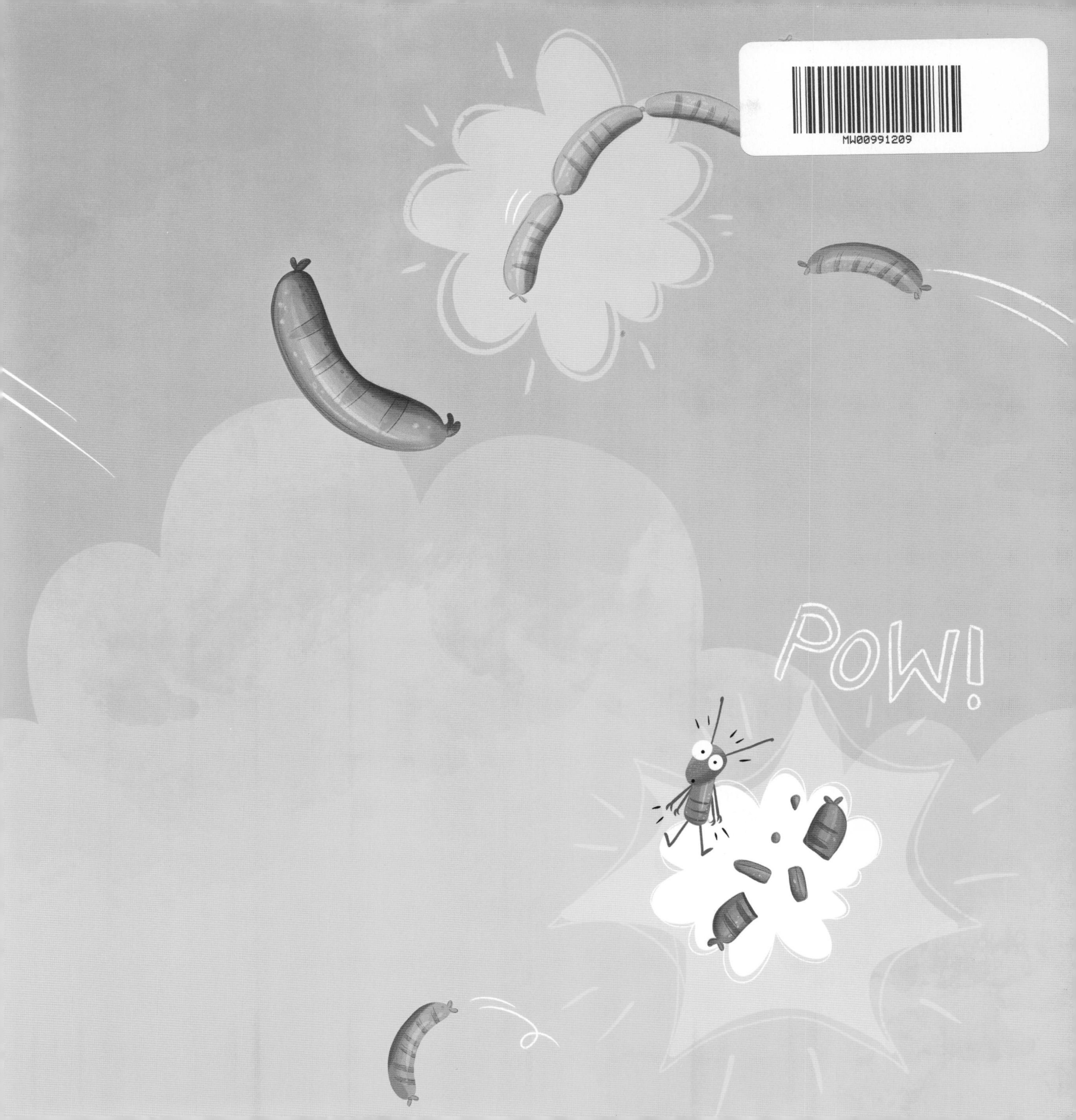
POW!

TO OUR TWO G.O.A.TS—K+J

FOR MY SIBLINGS DANA, TRENT, AND GEMMA AND OUR ENDLESS QUEST TO BE THE GOAT OF THE FAMILY—RC

Originally published by Scholastic Australia in 2023.

Library of Congress Cataloging-in-Publication Data Available
ISBN 978-1-5461-2726-0

10 9 8 7 6 5 4 3 2 1 24 25 26 27 28

Printed in China 127
This edition first printing, September 2024

G.O.A.T.

GREATEST OF ALL TIME

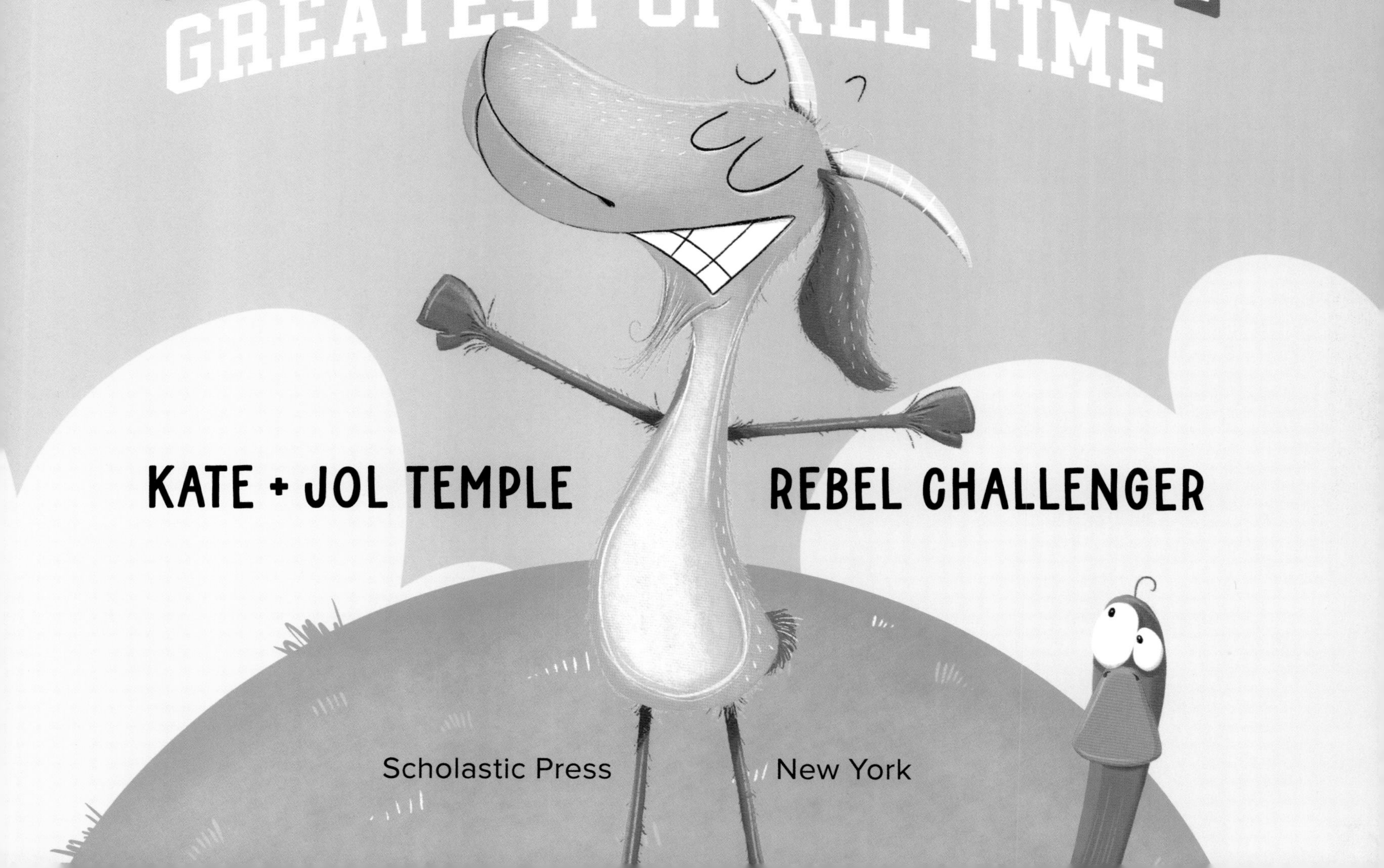

KATE + JOL TEMPLE

REBEL CHALLENGER

Scholastic Press New York

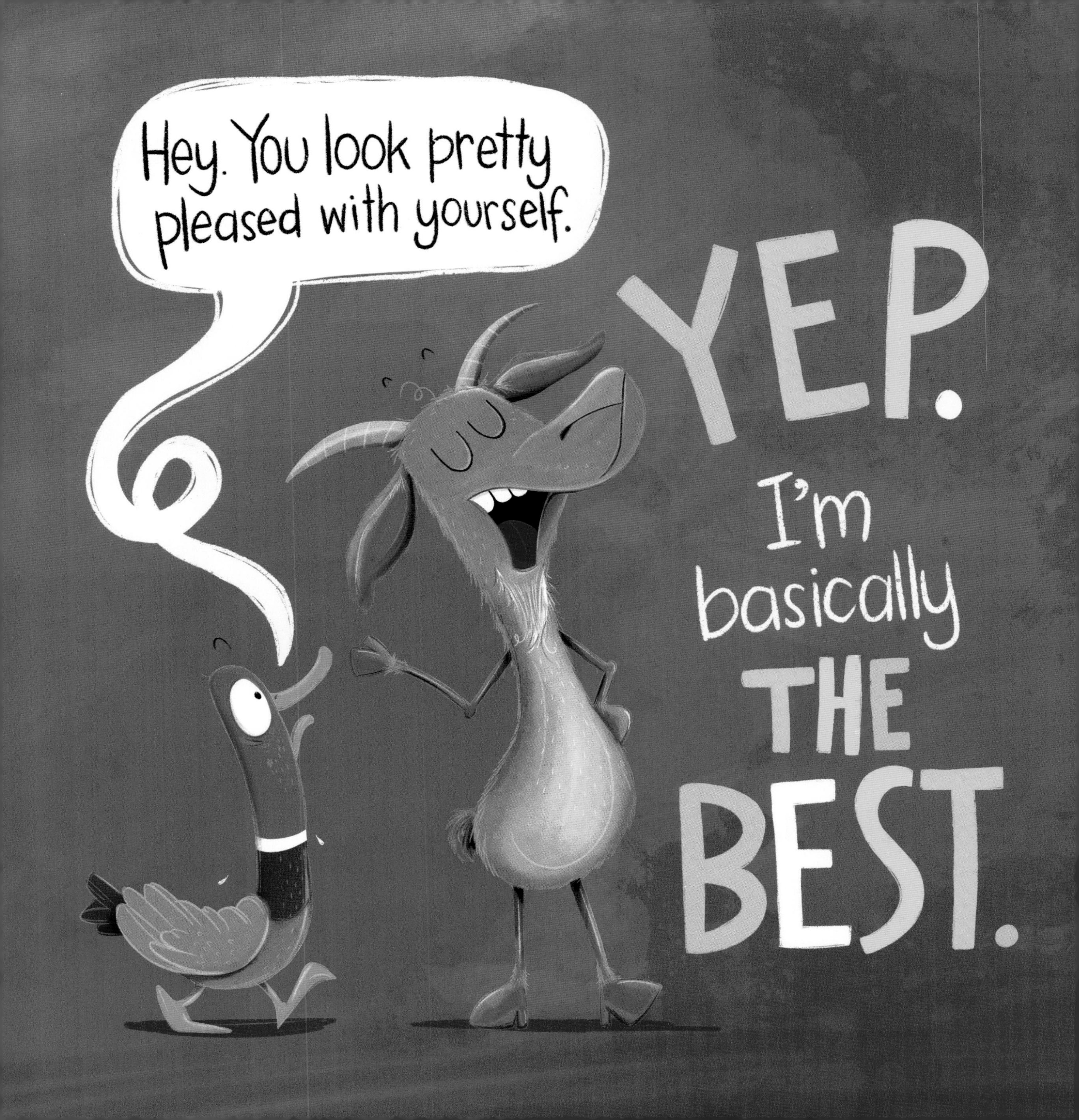
Hey. You look pretty pleased with yourself.
YEP.
I'm basically THE BEST.

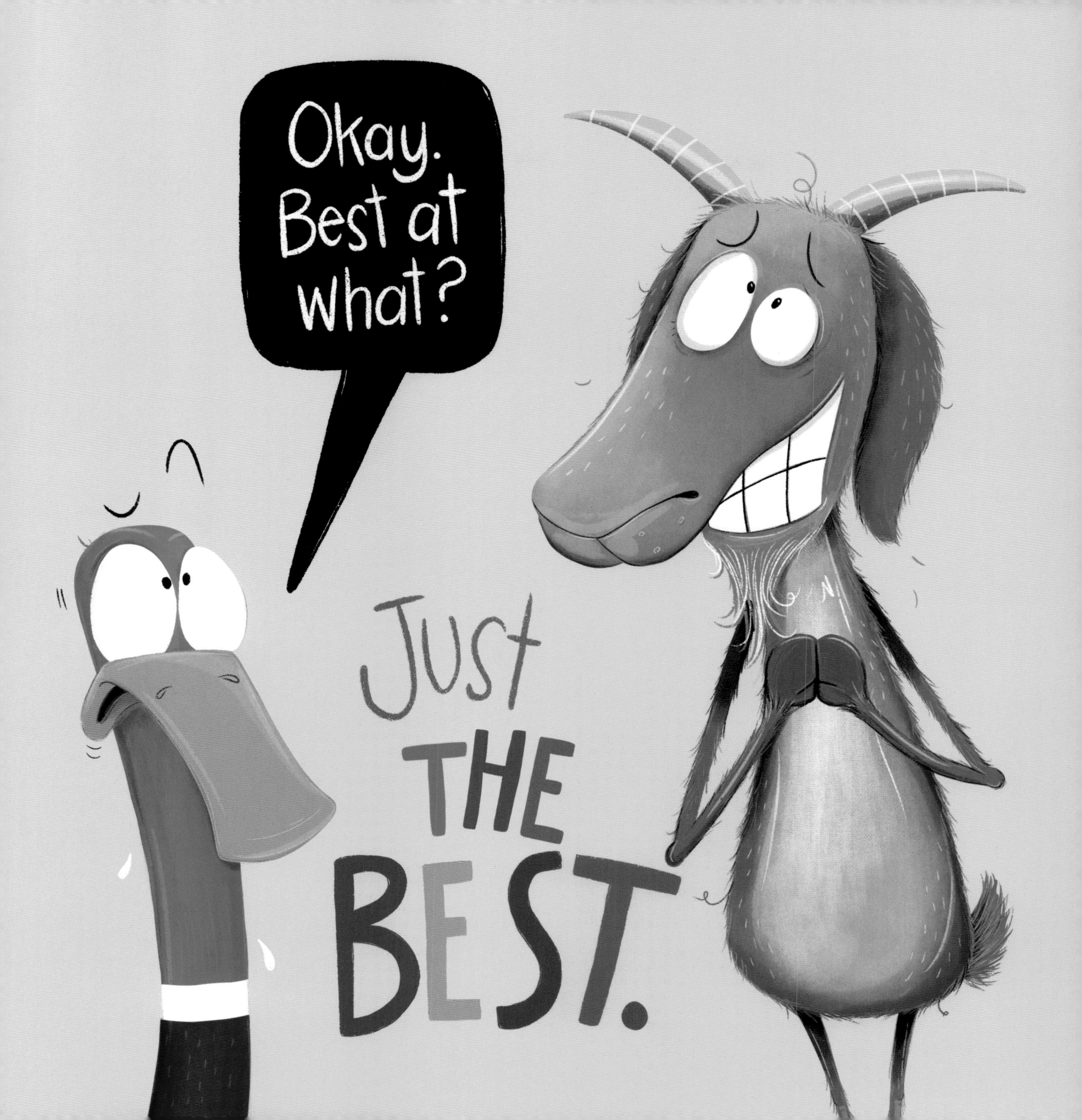
Okay. Best at what?
Just THE BEST.

Um...
okay...

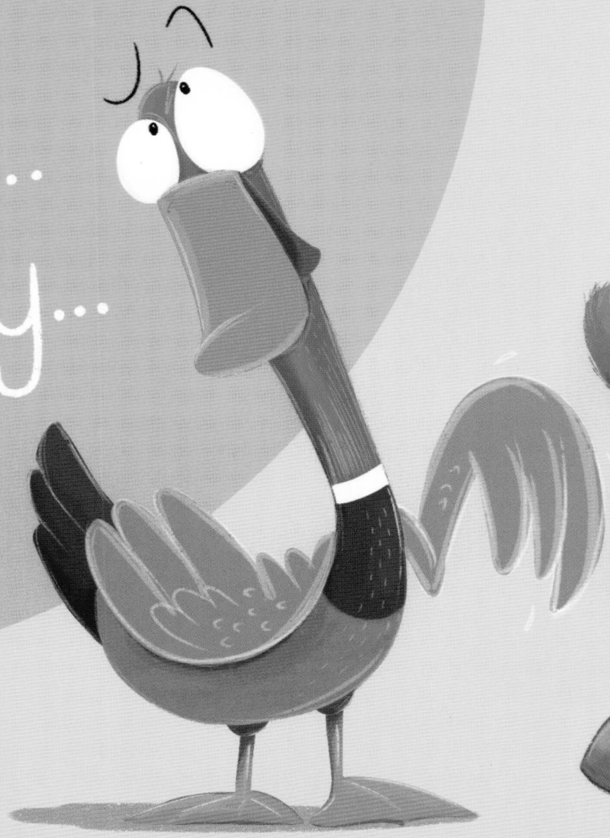

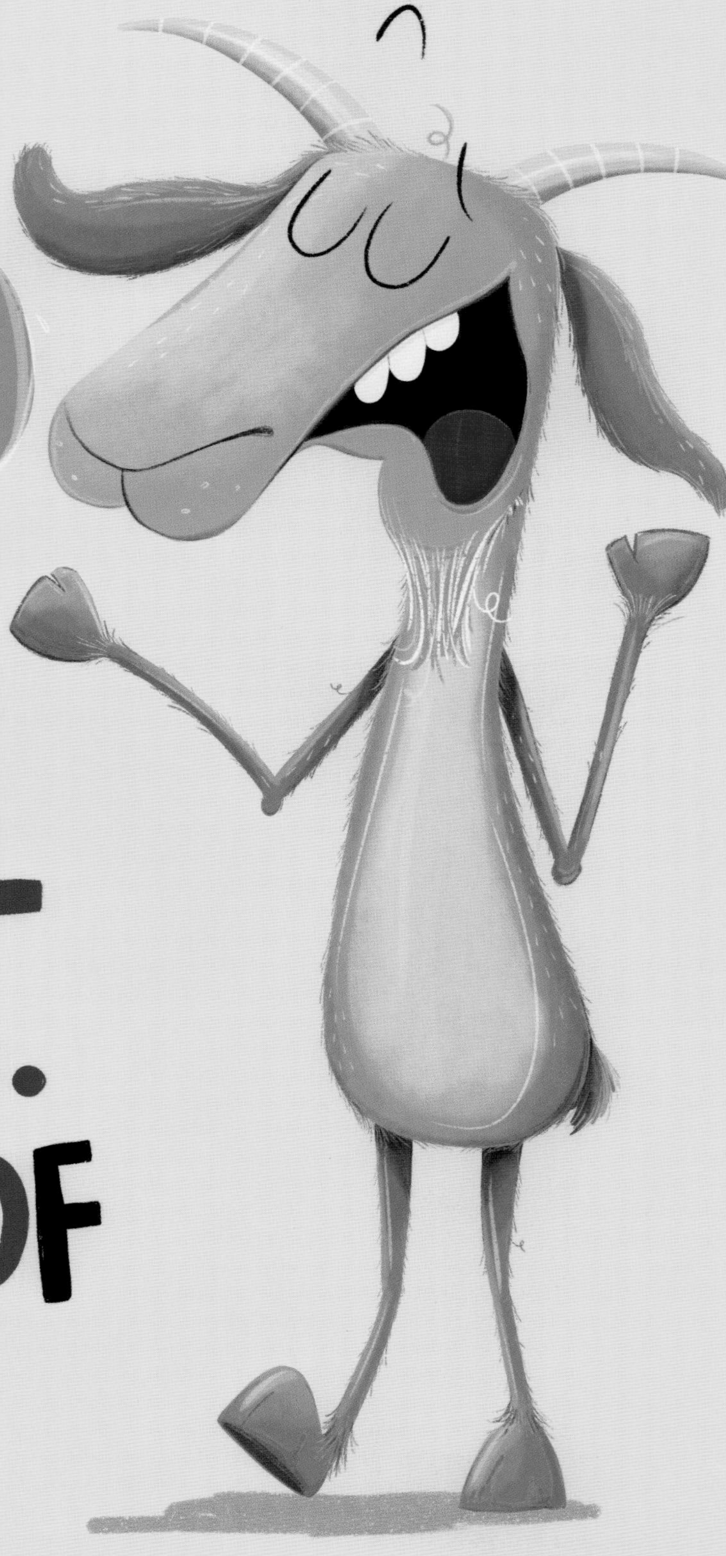

See?

G.O.A.T.

GREATEST OF ALL TIME.

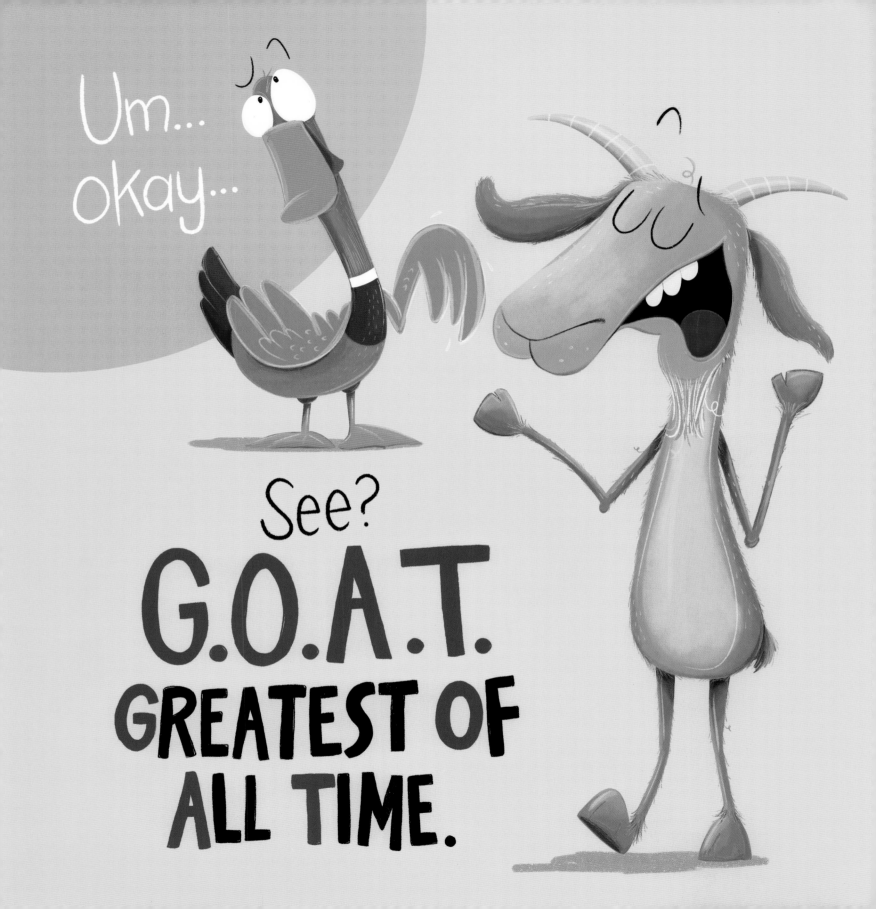

I thought it stood for

GOBBLES OATS AND TIRES?

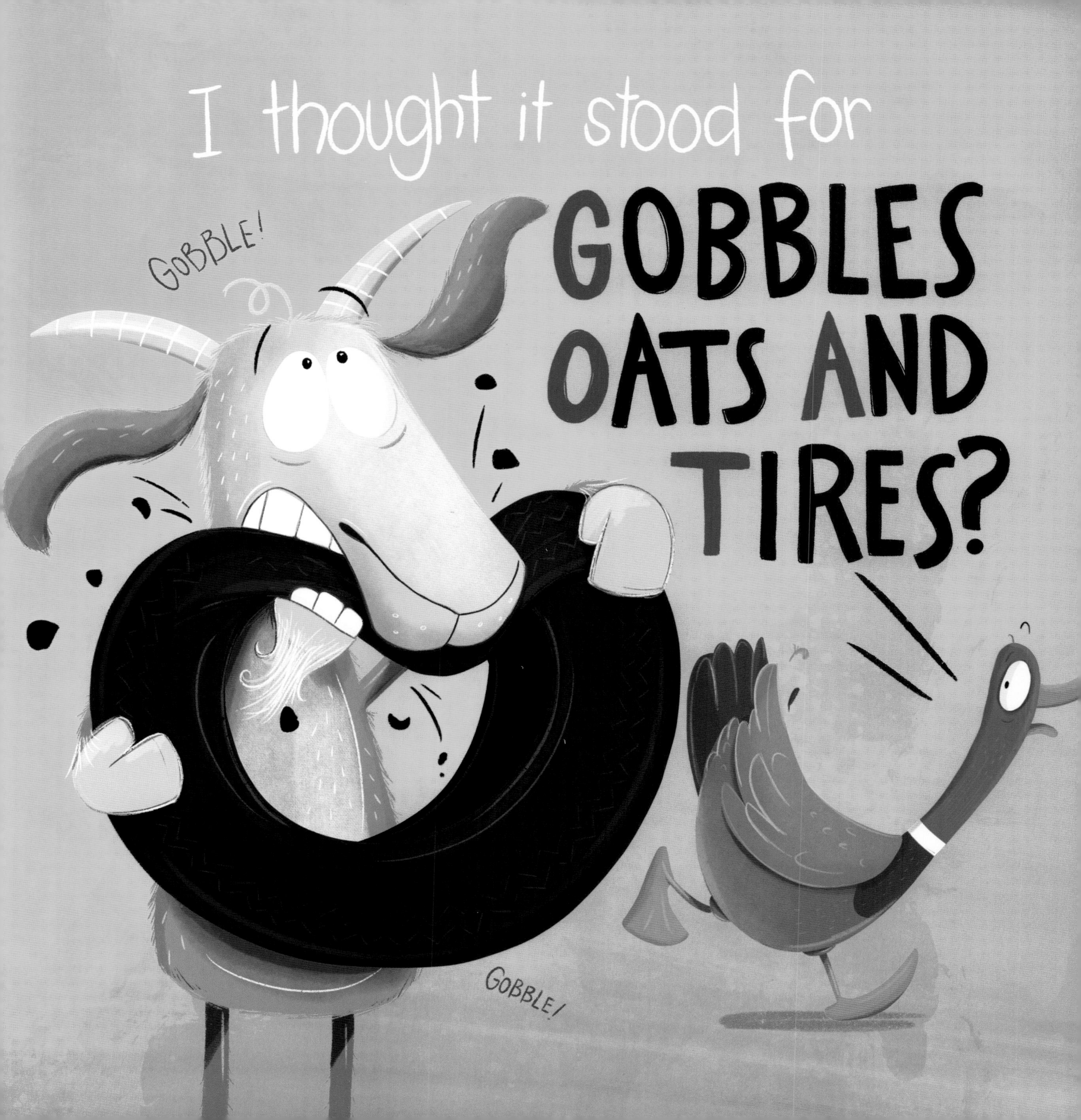
GOBBLE!
GOBBLE!

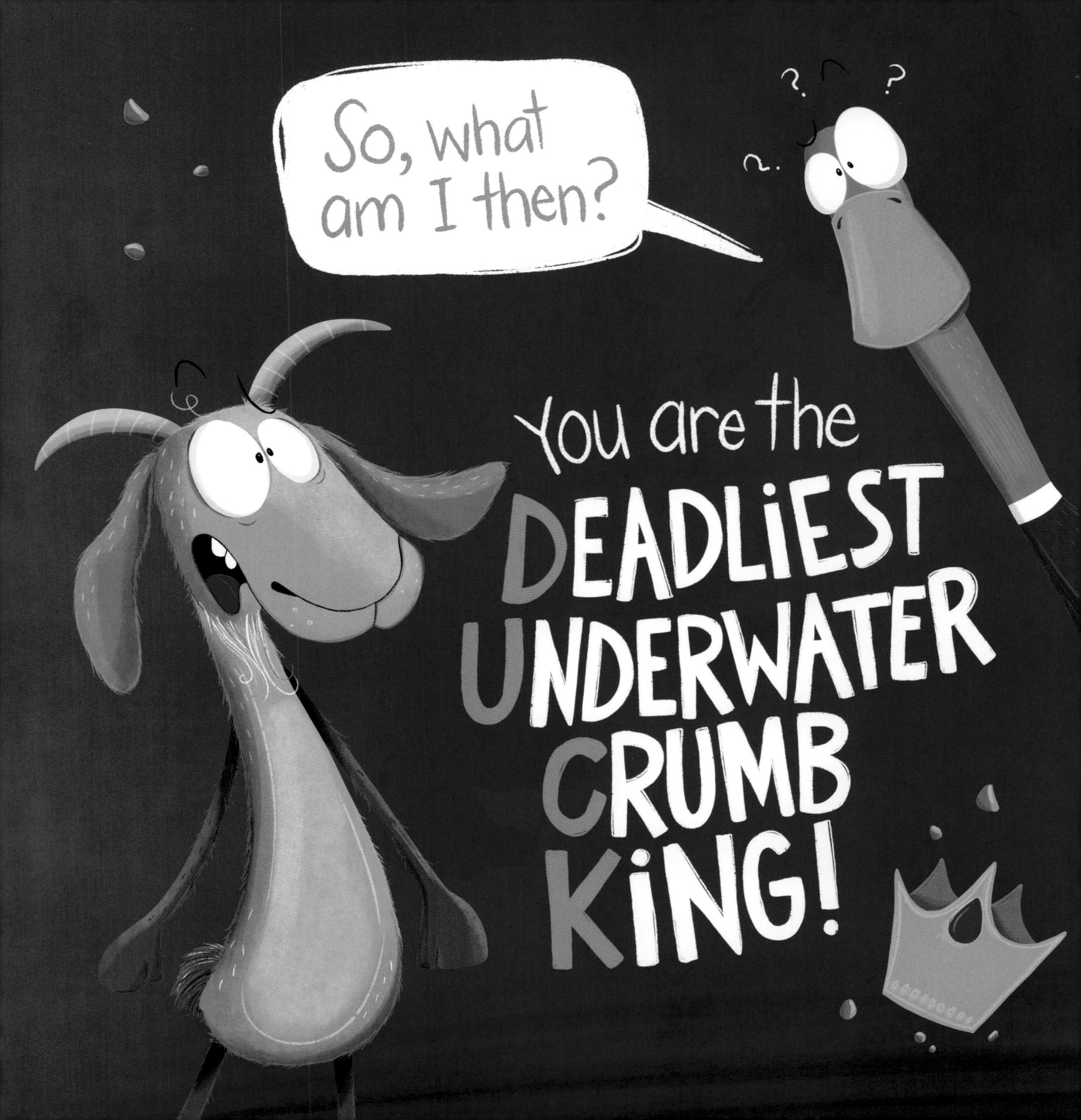

So, what am I then?
?
?
?
You are the
DEADLIEST
UNDERWATER
CRUMB
KiNG!

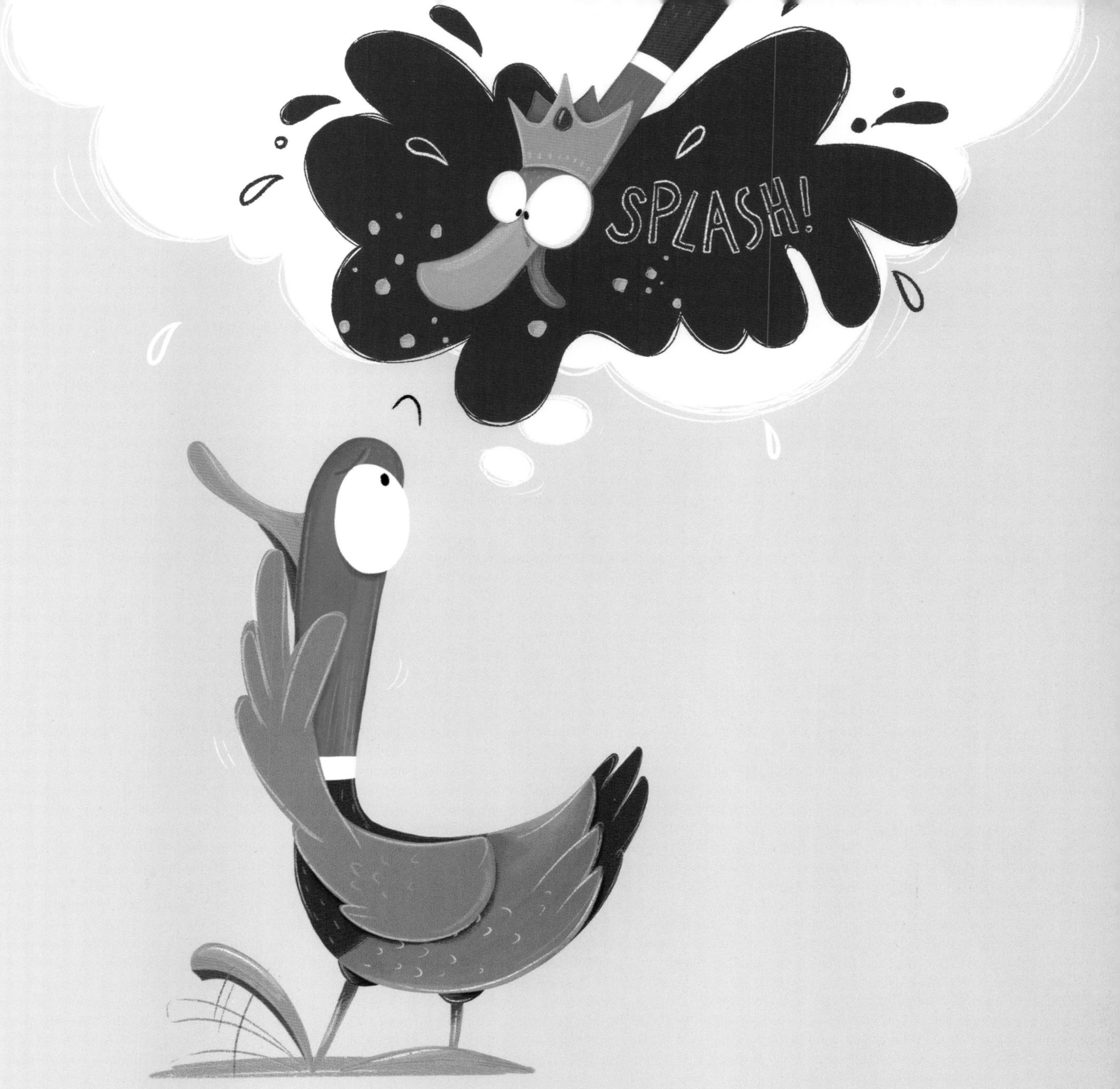
SPLASH!

Well, I DO like to eat breadcrumbs underwater...

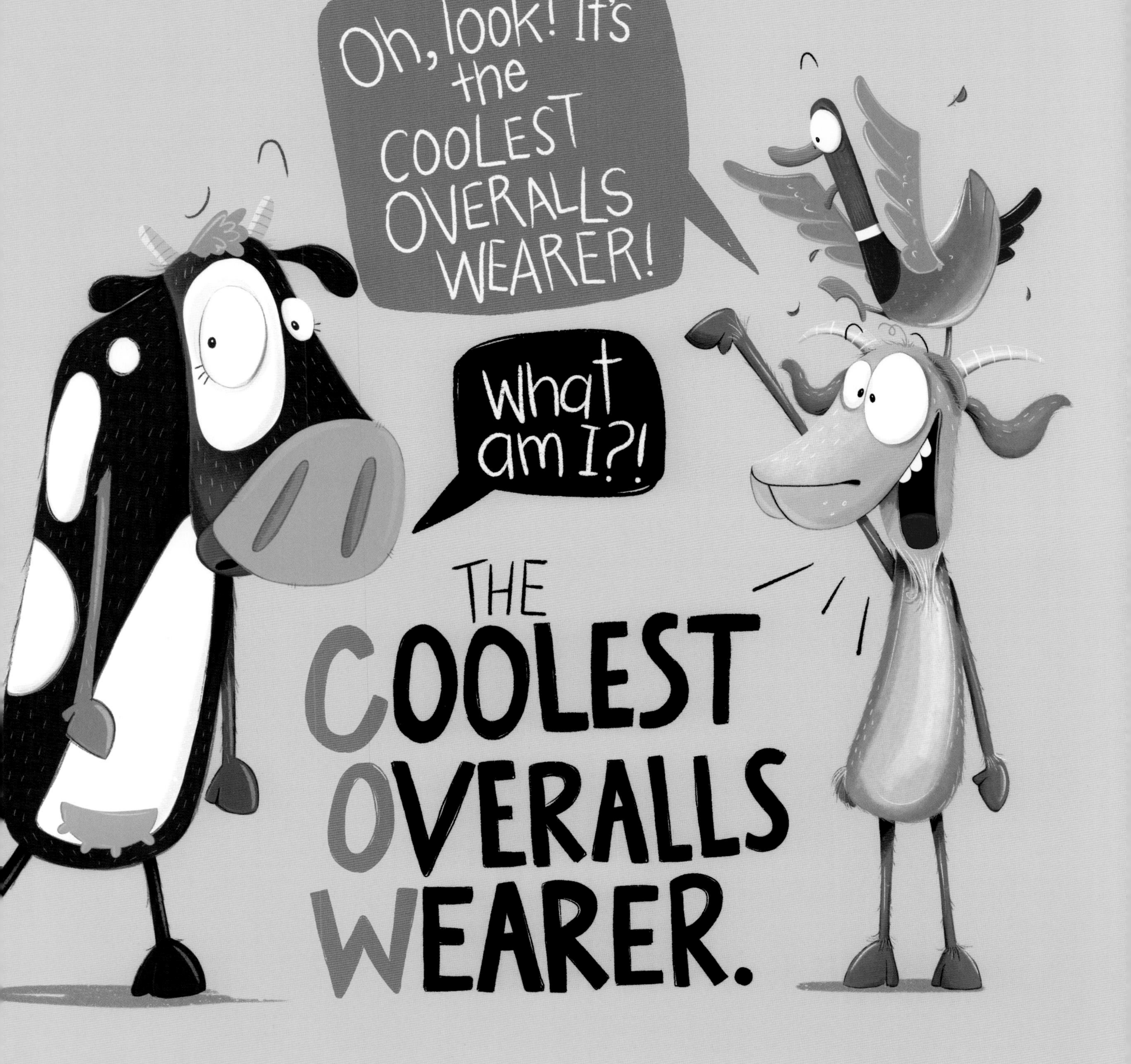
Oh, look! It's the COOLEST OVERALLS WEARER!
What am I?!
THE COOLEST OVERALLS WEARER.

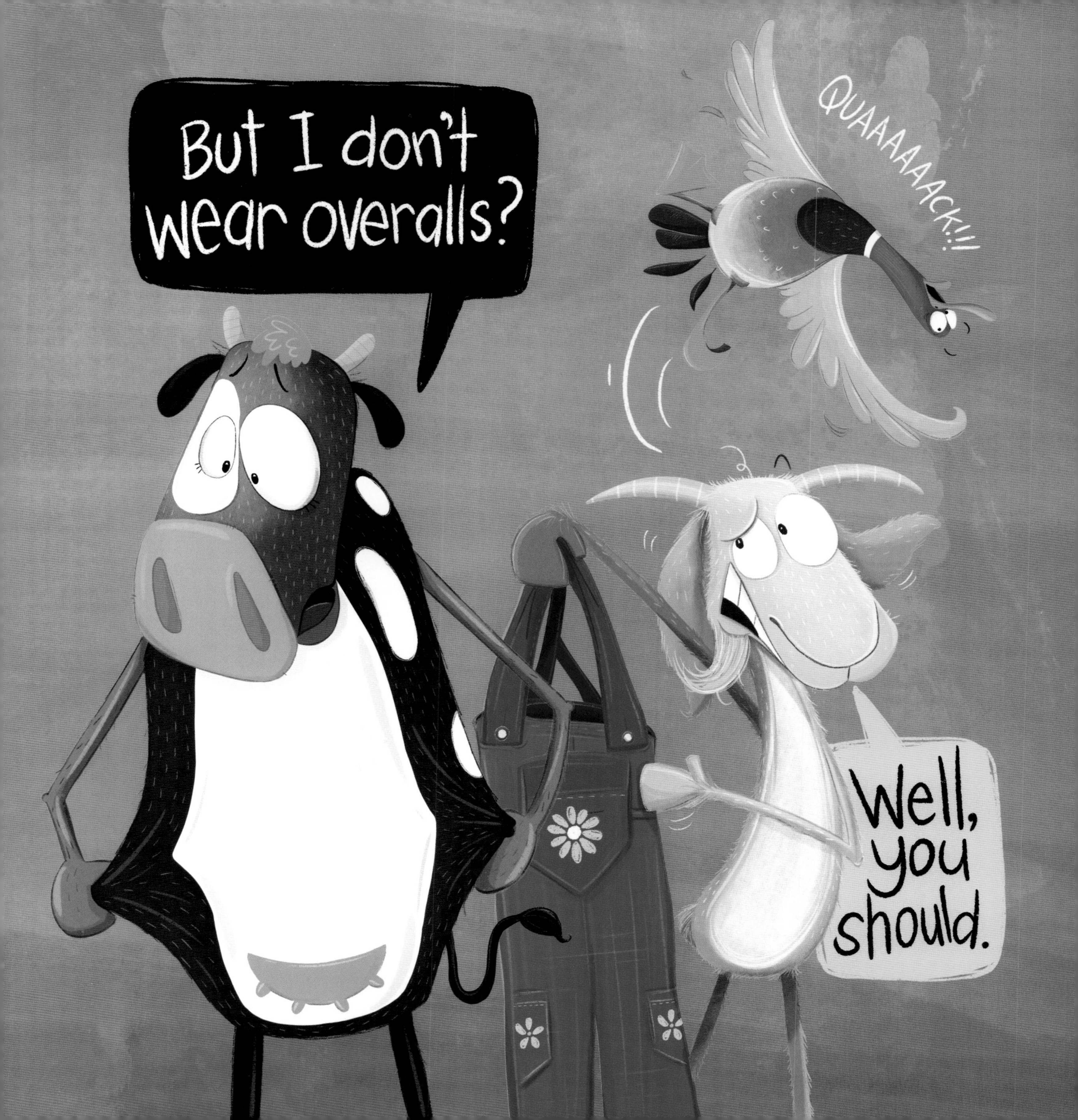
But I don't wear overalls?
QUAAAAAACK!!!
Well, you should.

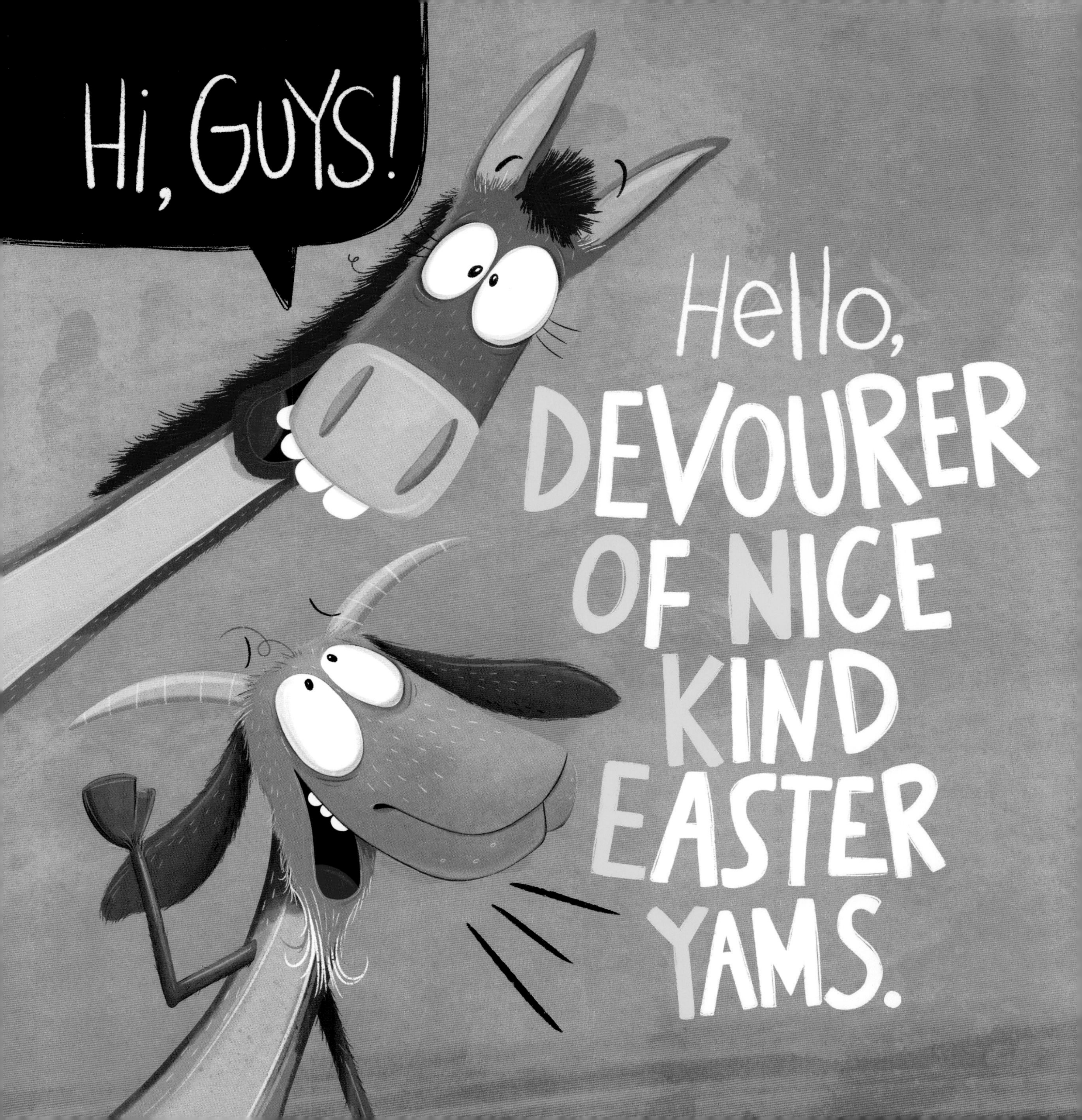
Hi, GUYS!
Hello,
DEVOURER OF NICE KIND EASTER YAMS.

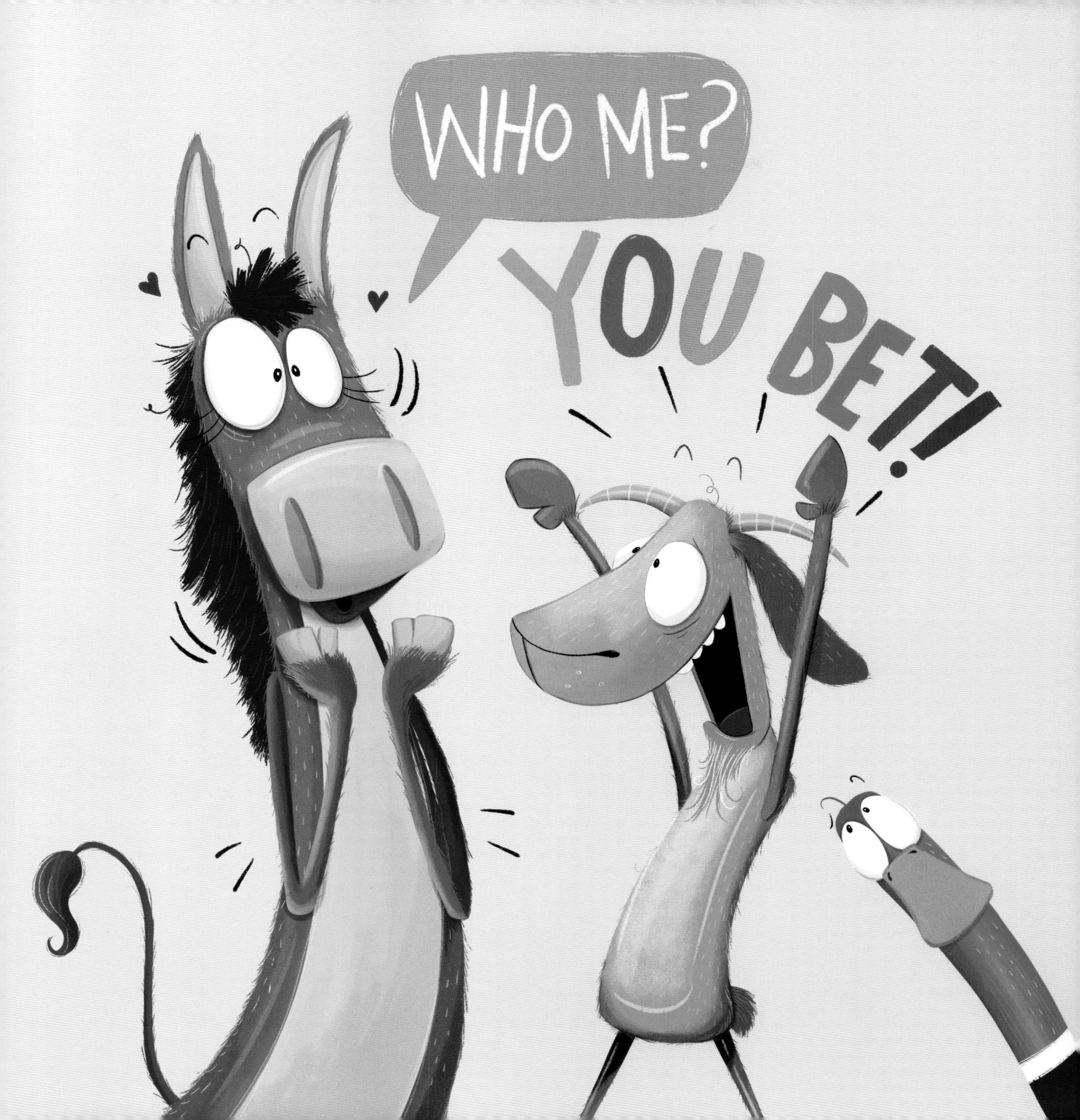
WHO ME?
YOU BET!

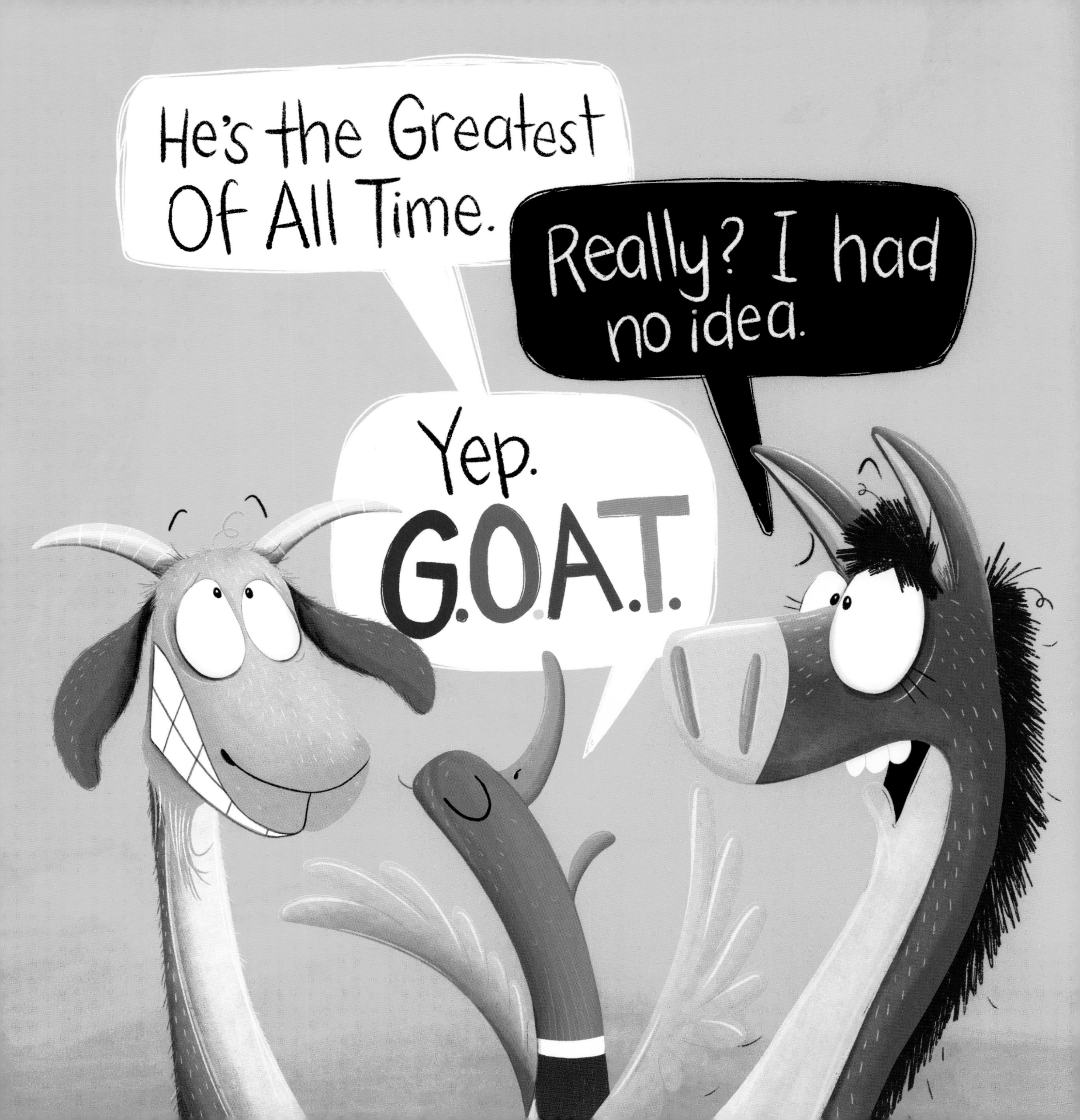
He's the Greatest Of All Time.
Really? I had no idea.
Yep.
G.O.A.T.

I thought that stood for

GRUNTS OFTEN AT TERMITES?

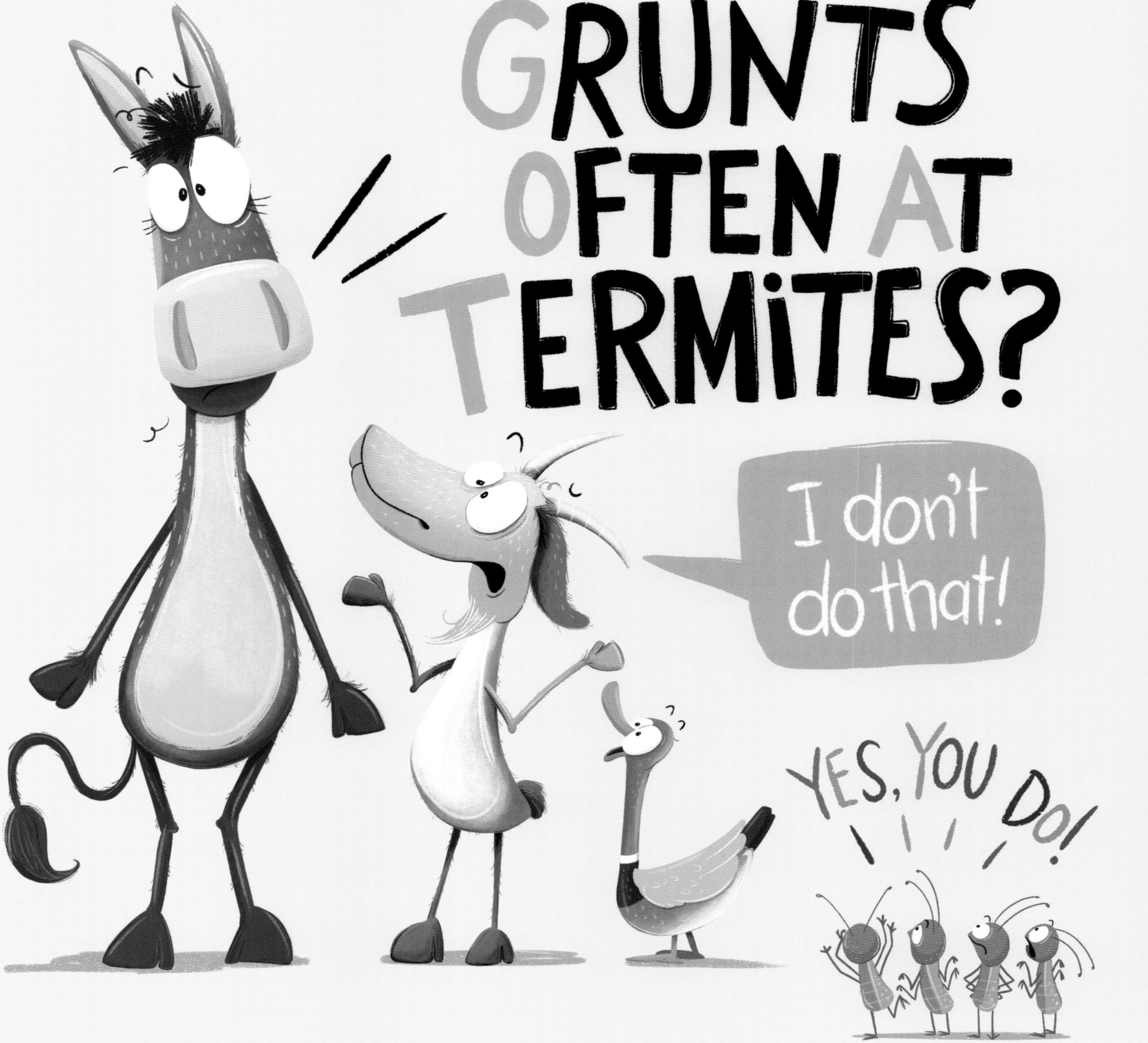
I don't do that!
YES, YOU DO!

Oh, it's you,

TERRIBLE EATERS REALLY MUST INVESTIGATE THE EXPLODING SAUSAGES.

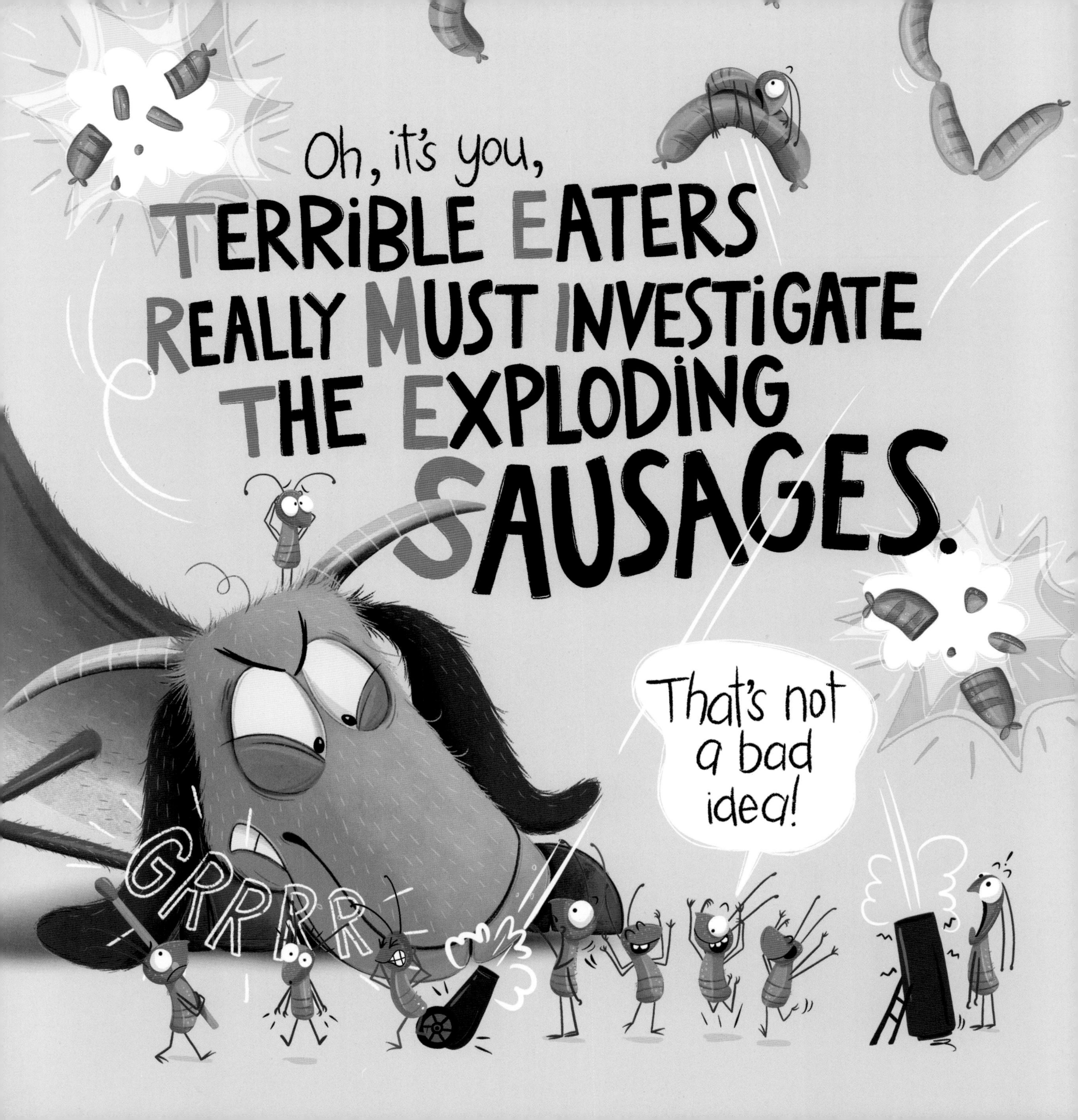
That's not a bad idea!
GRRRR

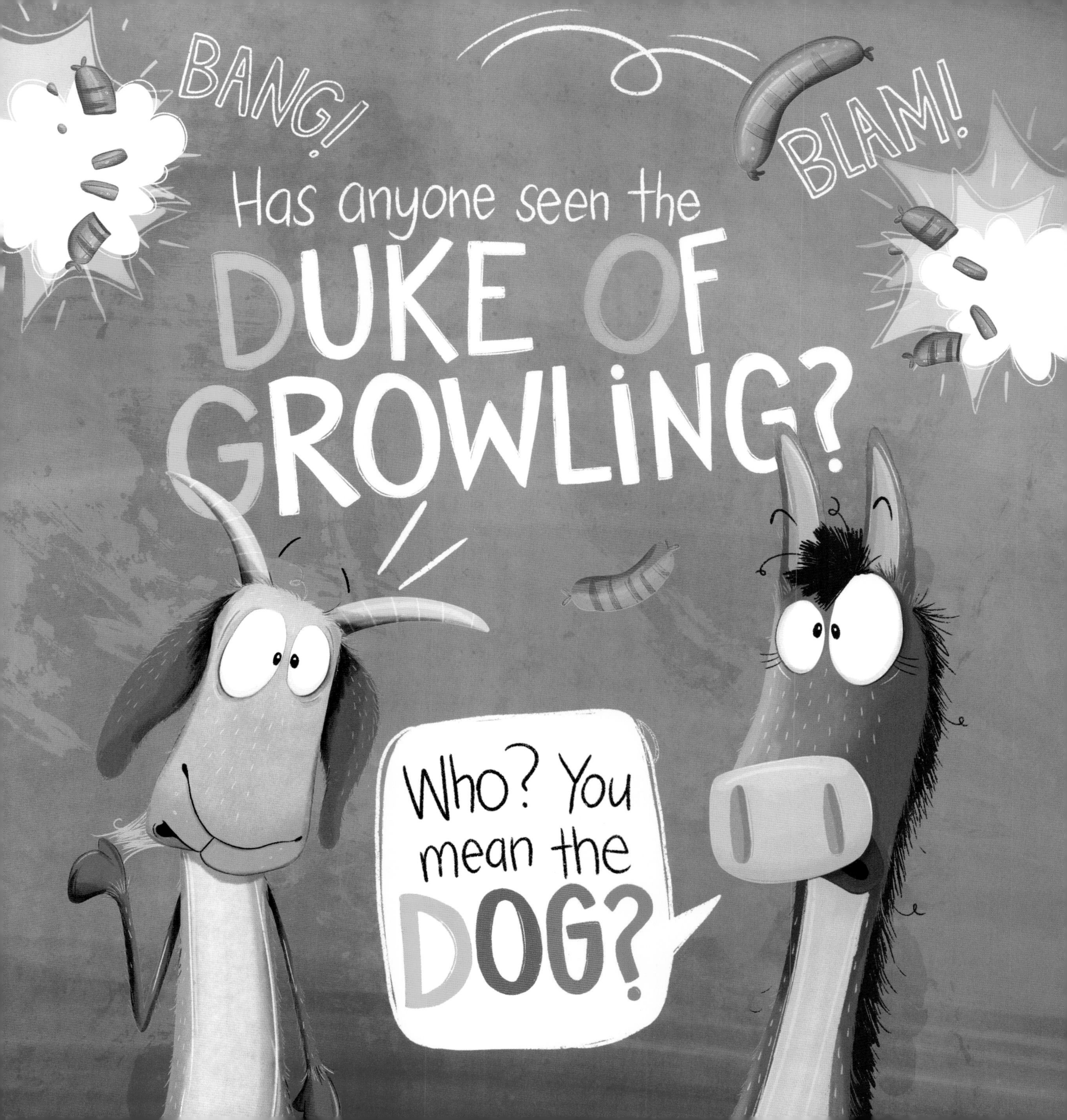
BANG!
BLAM!
Has anyone seen the DUKE OF GROWLING?
Who? You mean the DOG?

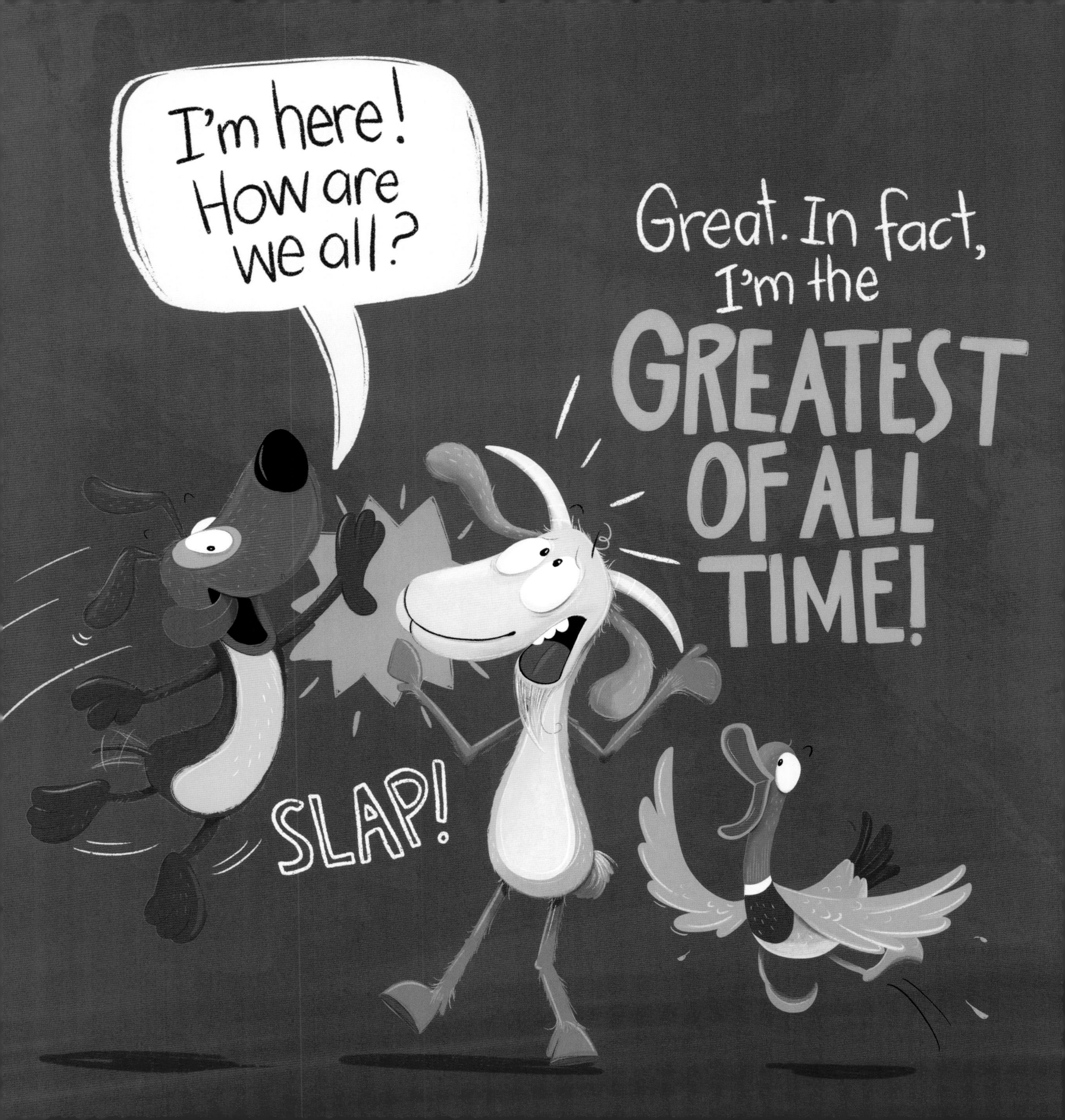
I'm here! How are we all?
Great. In fact, I'm the GREATEST OF ALL TIME!
SLAP!

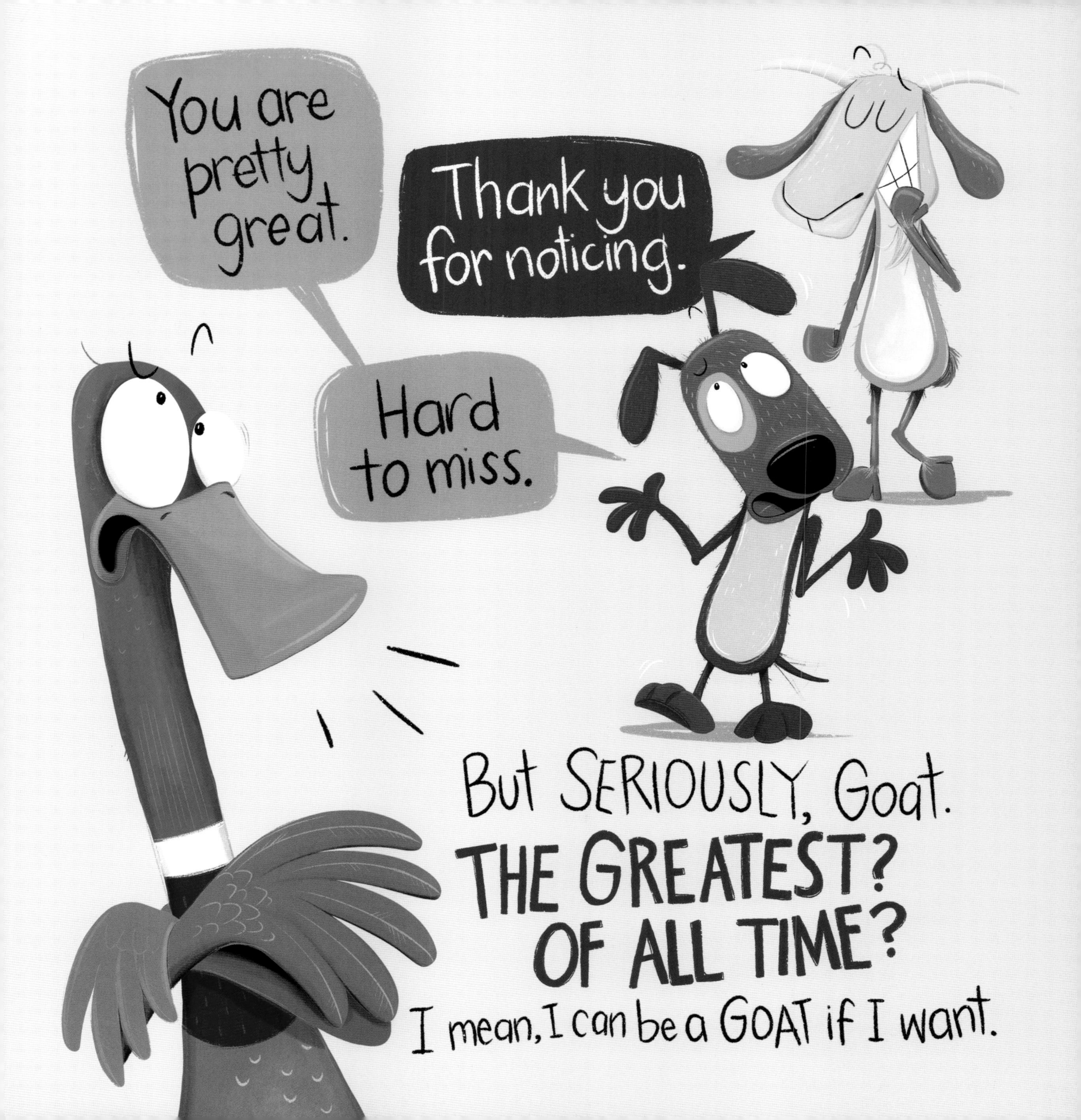
You are pretty great.
Thank you for noticing.
Hard to miss.
But SERIOUSLY, Goat.
THE GREATEST? OF ALL TIME?
I mean, I can be a GOAT if I want.

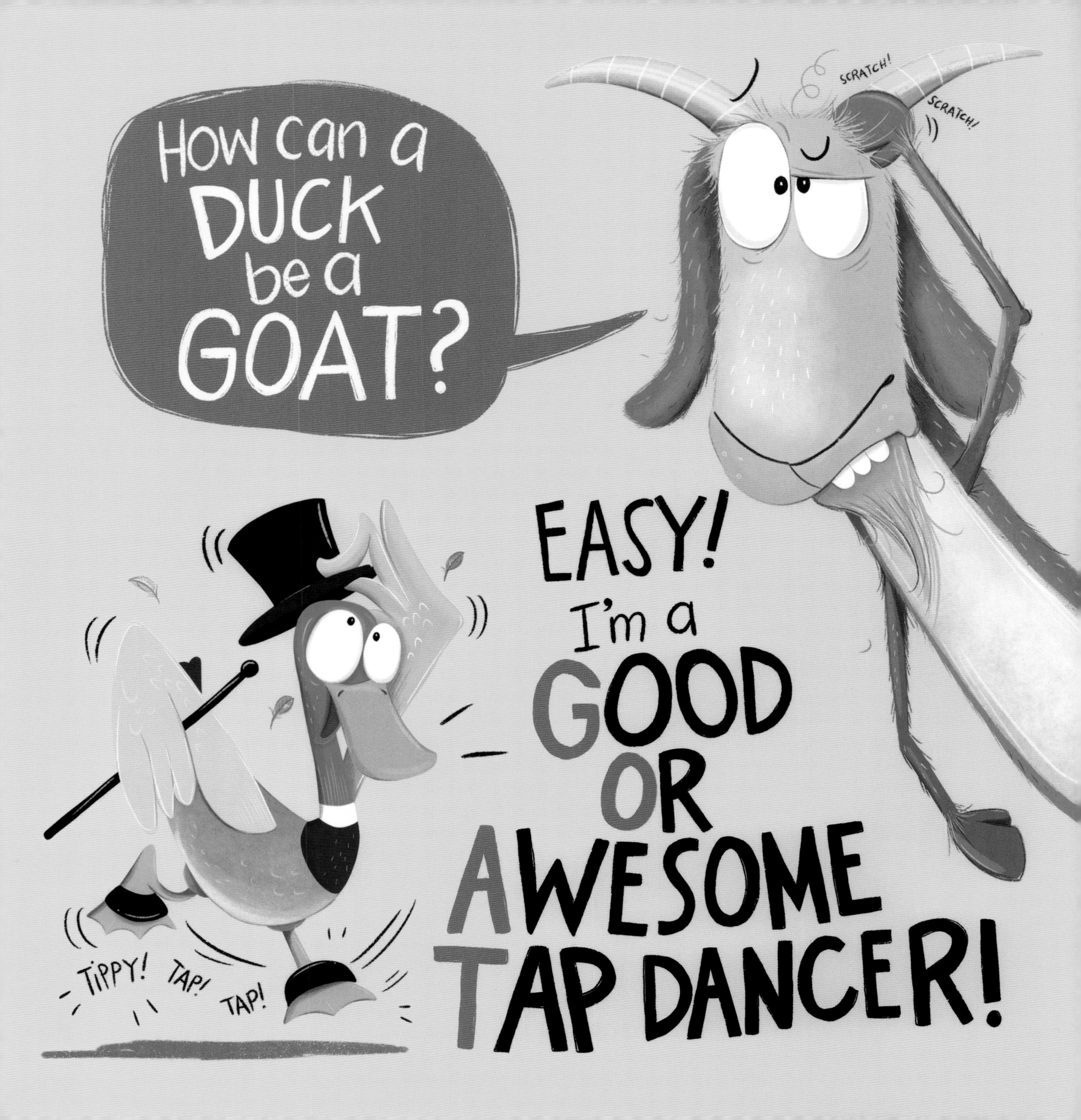
How can a DUCK be a GOAT?
SCRATCH!
SCRATCH!
EASY! I'm a GOOD OR AWESOME TAP DANCER!
TIPPY! TAP! TAP!

OooH! Yes. I'm a GOAT, too!

GORGEOUS OCTOPUS ARM TWiSTER.

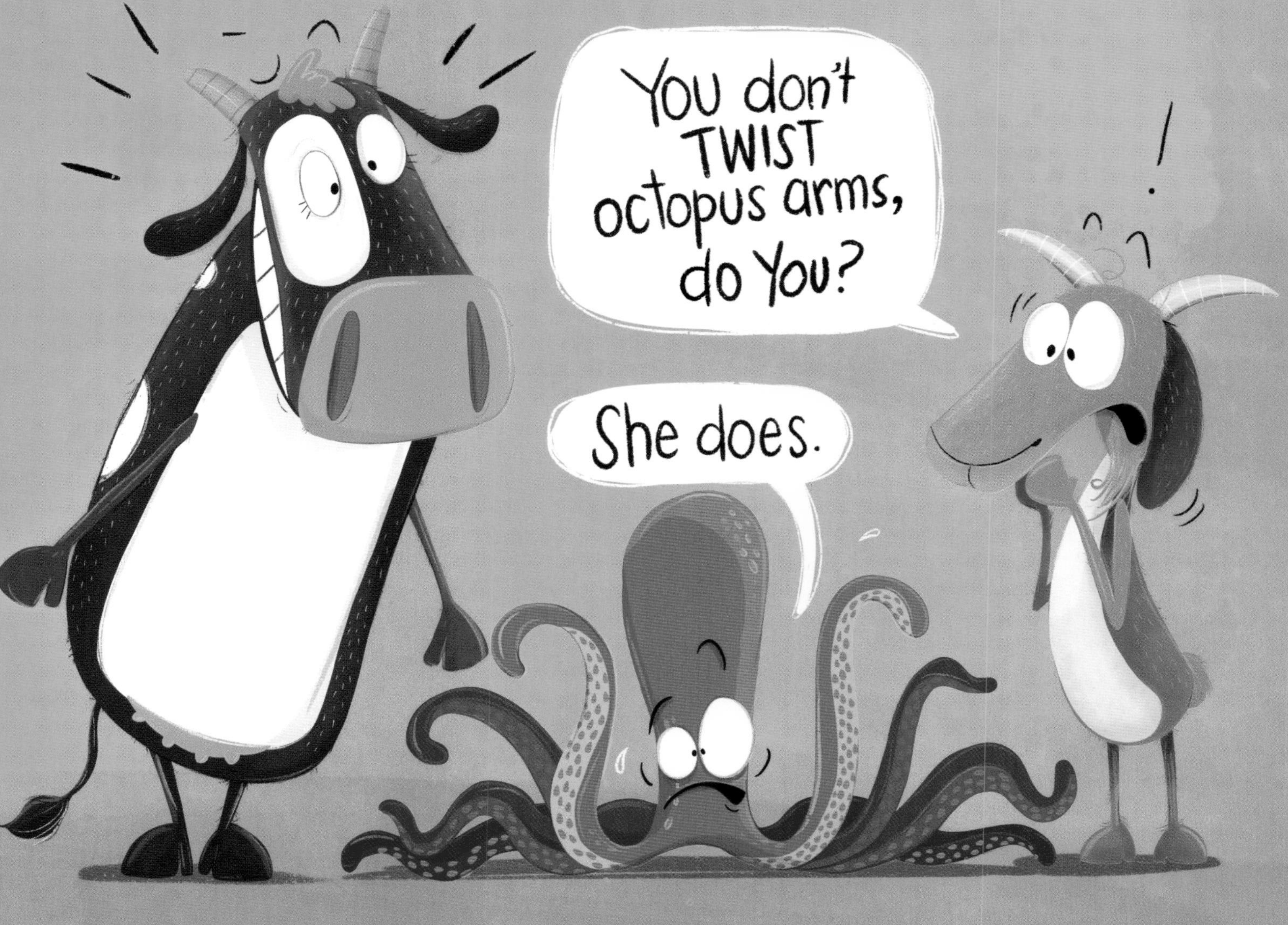

You don't TWIST octopus arms, do You?
She does.

Look, guys, I'm a GOAT, too!

GALLOPS ON ANY TABLE.

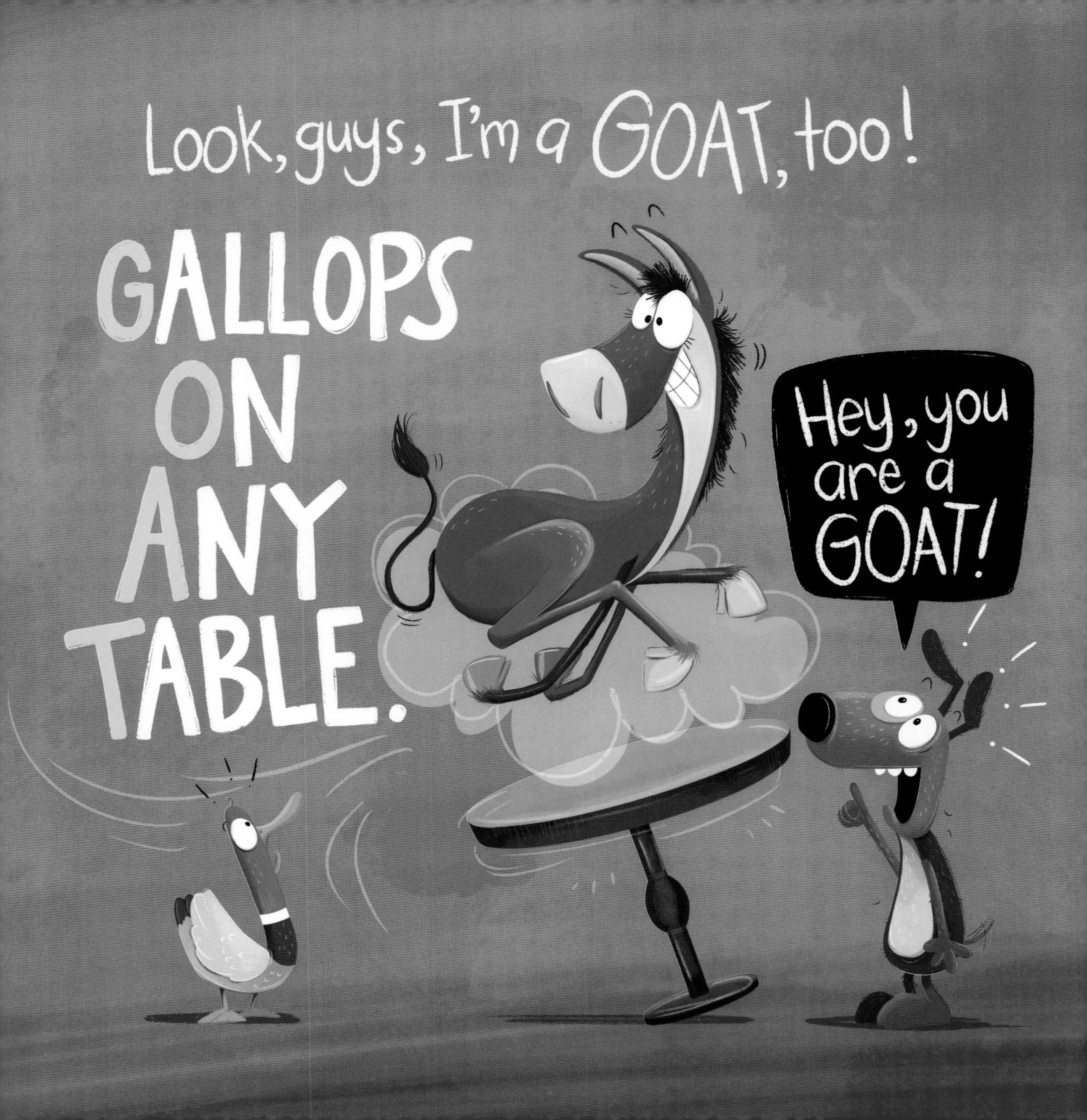
Hey, you are a GOAT!

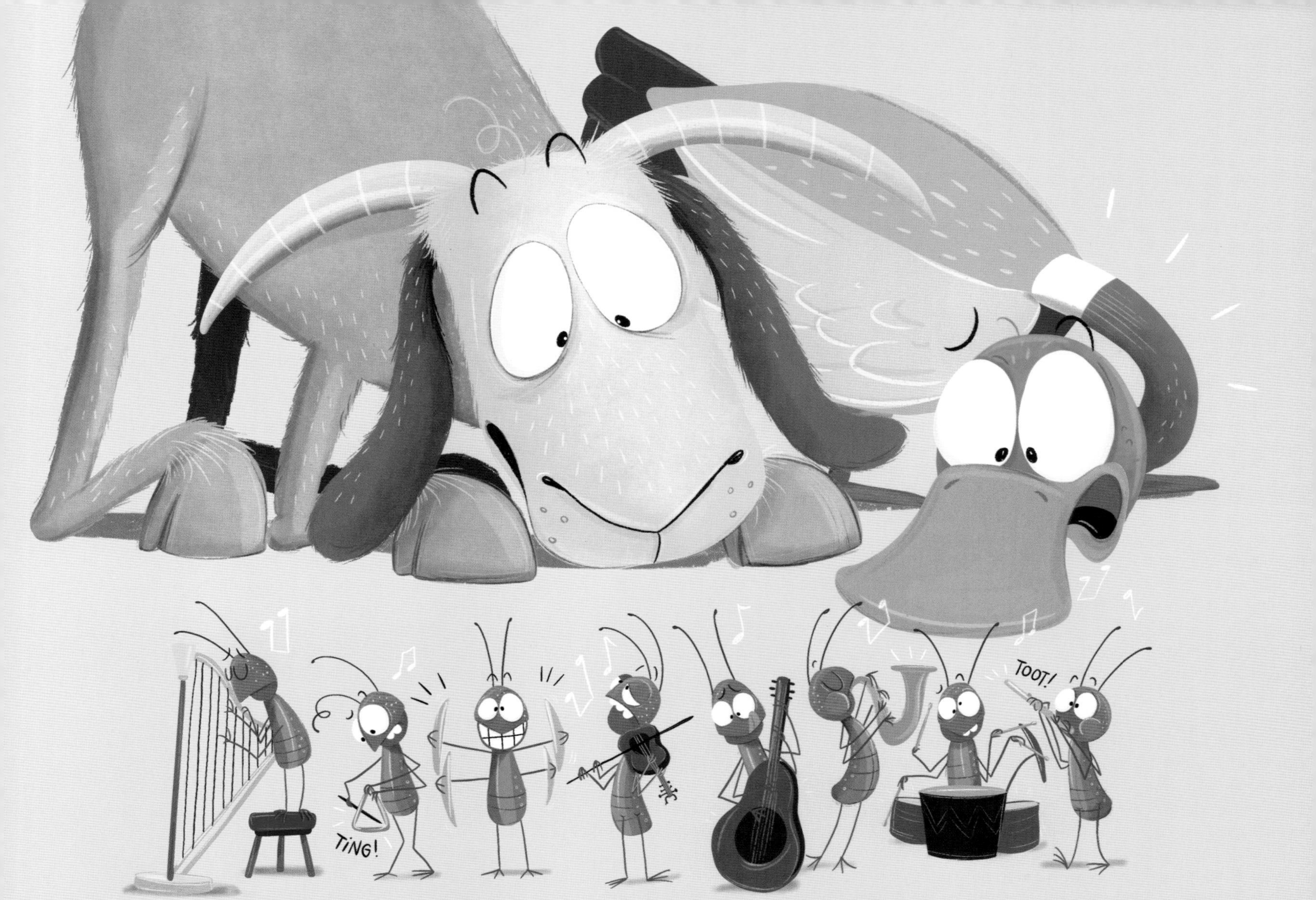
TOOT!
TING!

And we're GOATS, too!

GRAND ORCHESTRAL AMAZING TALENT.

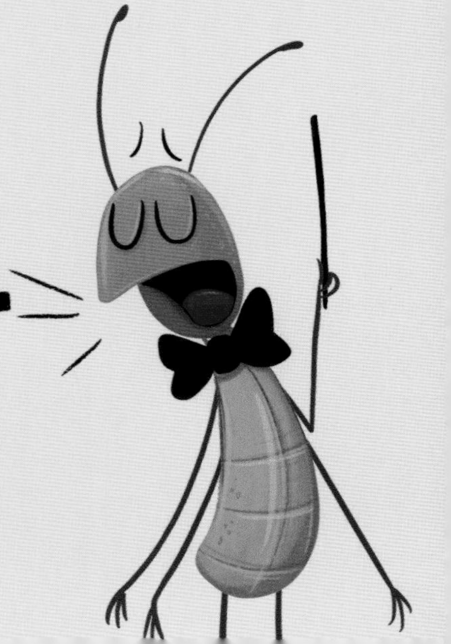

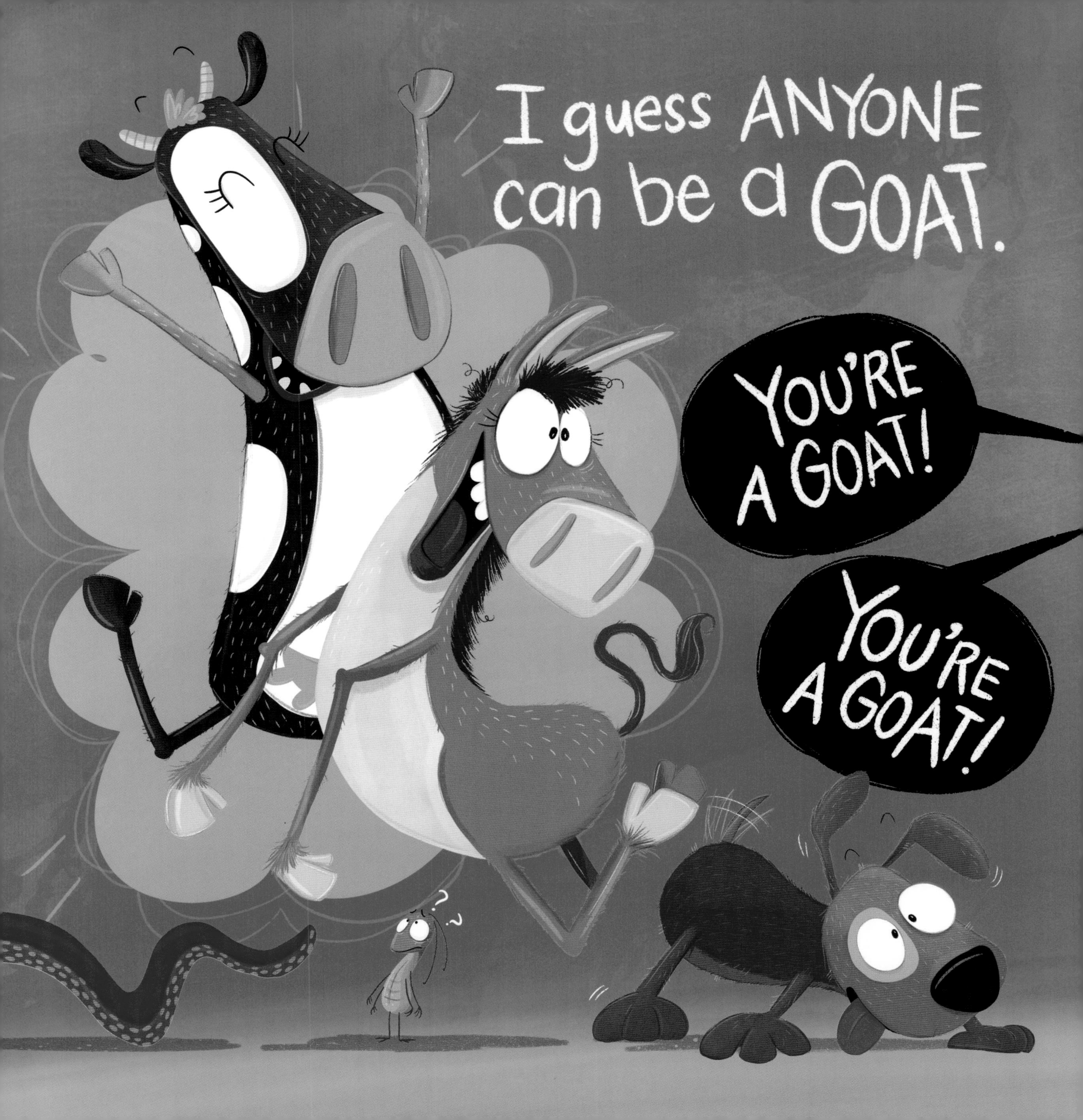
I guess ANYONE can be a GOAT.
YOU'RE A GOAT!
YOU'RE A GOAT!

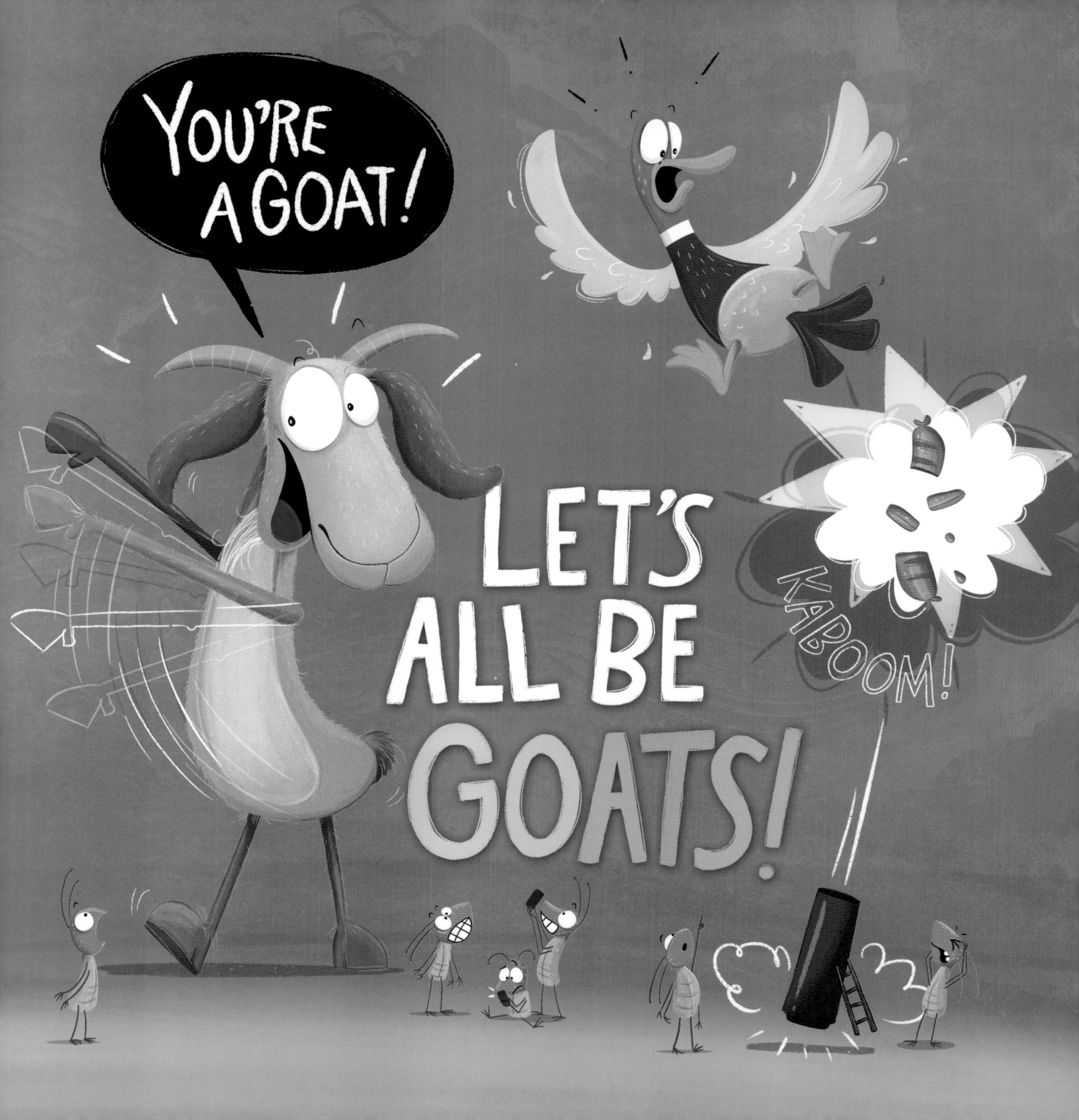
YOU'RE A GOAT!
LET'S ALL BE GOATS!
KABOOM!

I'll pass.

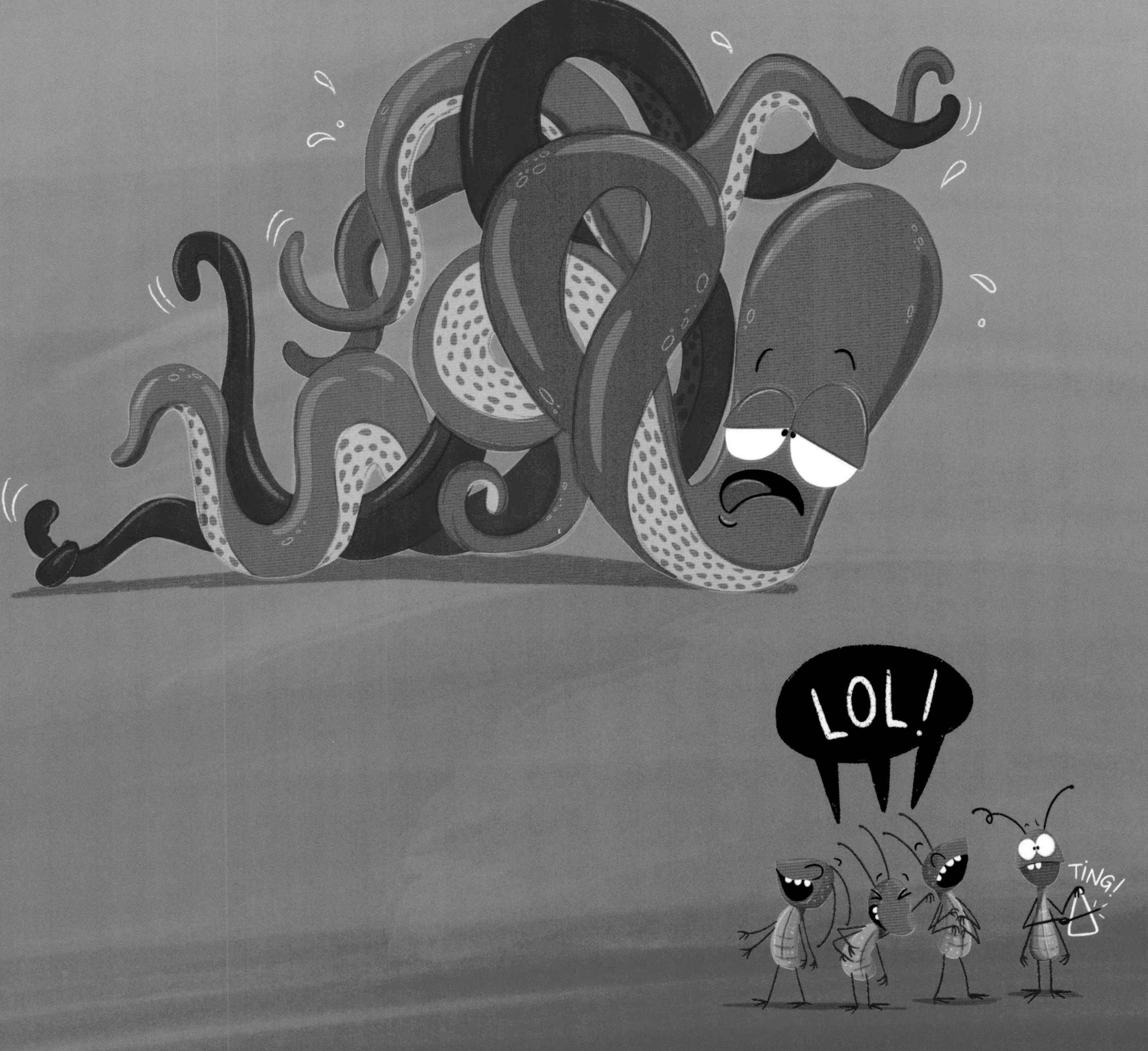
LOL!
TING!

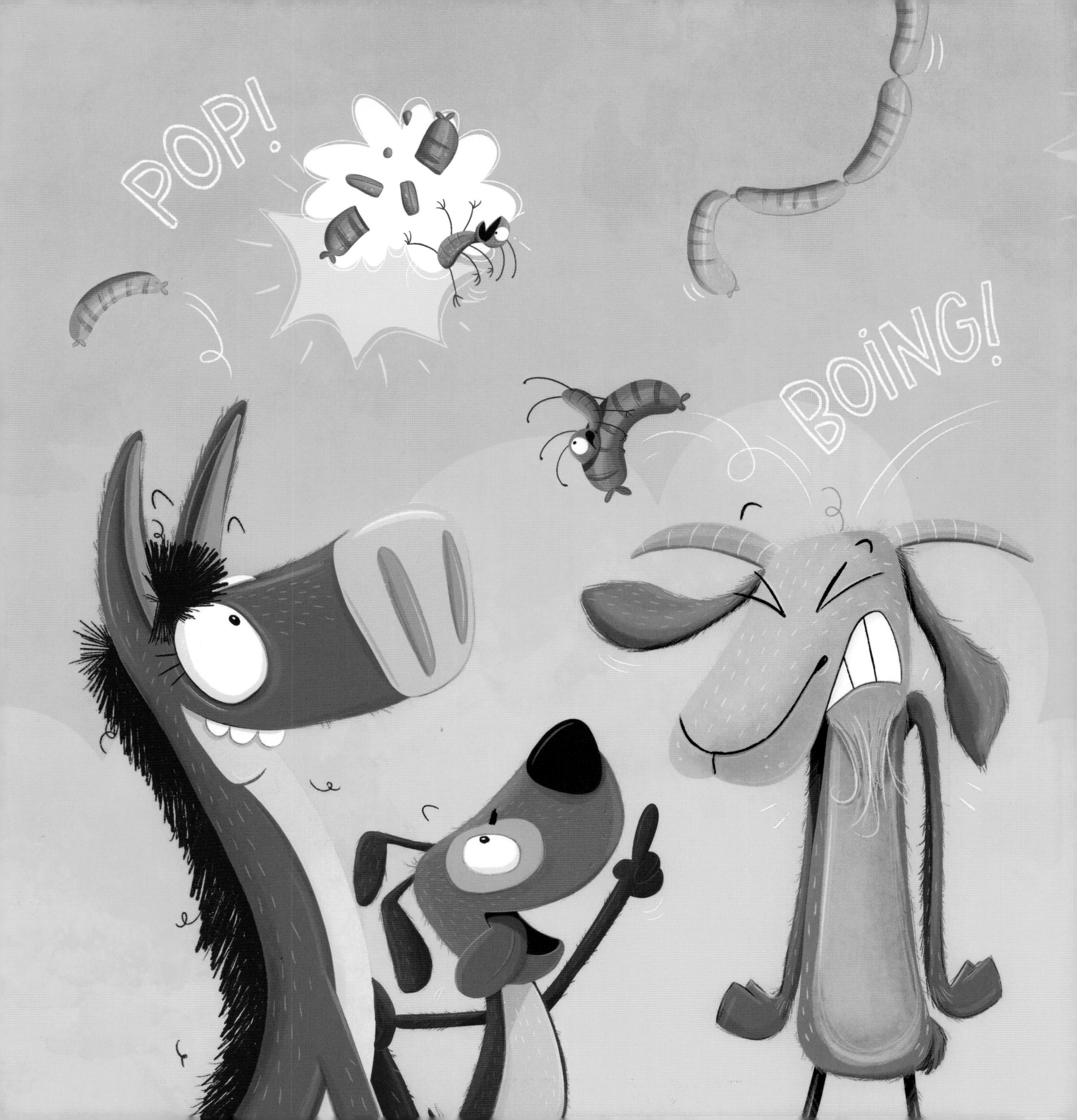
POP!
BOING!